WAKE UP

HOUSE!

Rooms
Full
of
Poems

by Dee Lillegard
illustrated by Don Carter

ALFRED A. KNOPF
New York

Wake Up House!
Just before dawn
House stretches
starts to yawn—

Bedroom Window

Sun rises
lights the sky
shines through the window's
open eye.

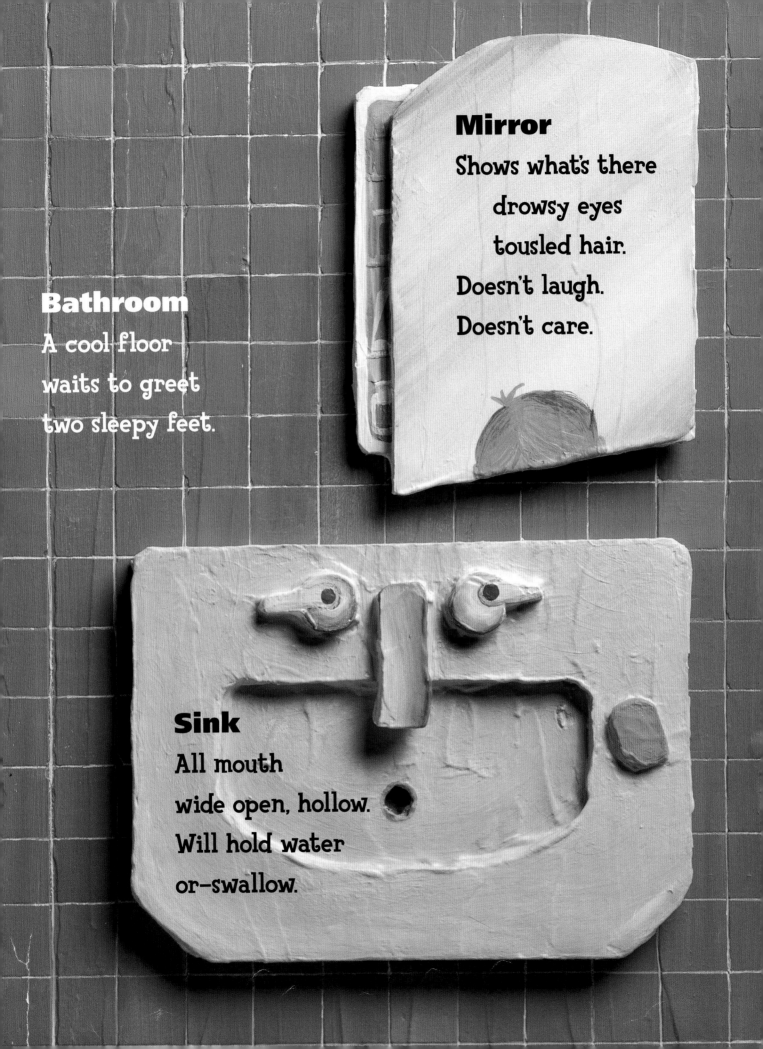

Bathroom

A cool floor
waits to greet
two sleepy feet.

Mirror

Shows what's there
drowsy eyes
tousled hair.
Doesn't laugh.
Doesn't care.

Sink

All mouth
wide open, hollow.
Will hold water
or–swallow.

Kitchen

Cabinets stretch.
Drawers yawn.
Morning, Kitchen!
Lights on!

Stove

Stalwart, sturdy,
on the spot.
Ready to heat up
pan or pot.

Refrigerator
Chilly but cheery
she opens wide,
happy to share
what she's got inside.

Broom
Look out!
There she goes!
Chasing crumbs
and oaty O's.

Washer

Heavy-duty dude
handles dirty duds
–with *suds!*

Dryer

When clothes are wet
and want to cry,
she warms them up
and tumbles them dry.

Stairs

Spiny back
of a stegosaur,
stretching itself
from floor to floor.

Doors

Flat out stop you
when they're closed.
Let you pass
when so disposed—

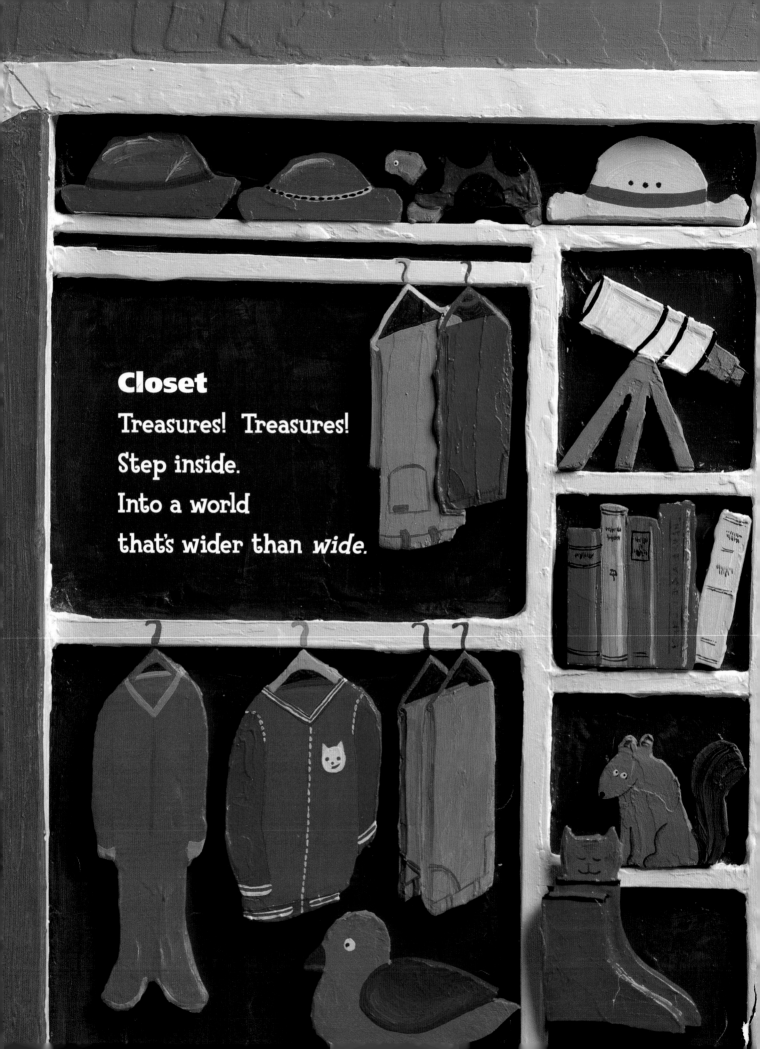

Closet

Treasures! Treasures!
Step inside.
Into a world
that's wider than *wide*.

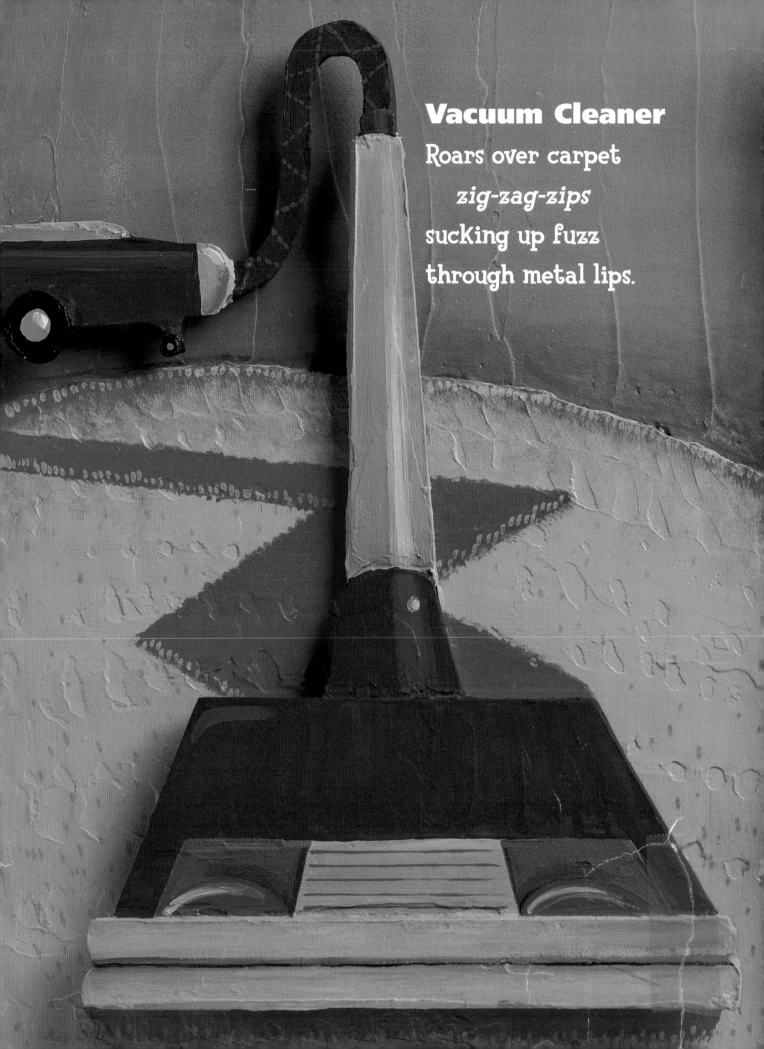

Vacuum Cleaner

Roars over carpet
zig-zag-zips
sucking up fuzz
through metal lips.

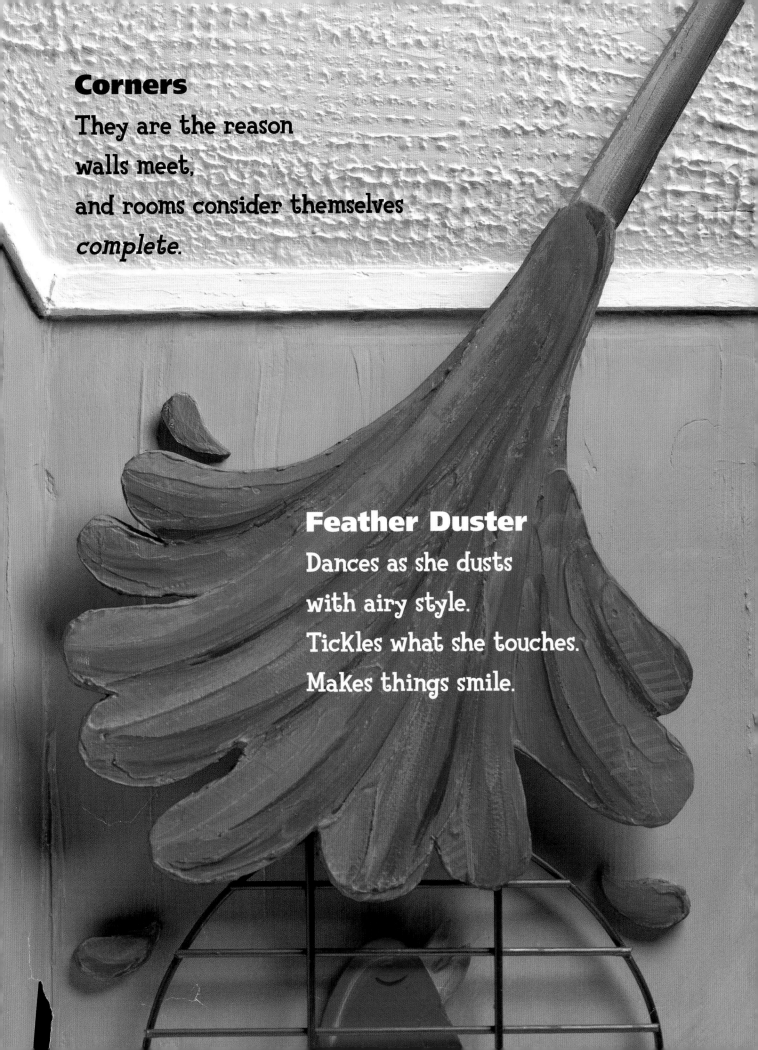

Corners

They are the reason
walls meet,
and rooms consider themselves
complete.

Feather Duster

Dances as she dusts
with airy style.
Tickles what she touches.
Makes things smile.

Rocking Chair

Rocker, Rocker
dear old soul
rock rock rock
but do not roll!

Tape Player

Feed him tapes,
he can't refuse.
He'll perform
the songs you choose.

Fan

A blur of blades
with chilling power.
Then a silent,
steel-petaled
flower.

Bookcase

Book out   book out
    space   space
Like missing teeth
in a smiling face.

The Shadow

The Shadow knows
where to fall
　in shrinking room
　on fading wall
wherever Sun
has ceased to call.

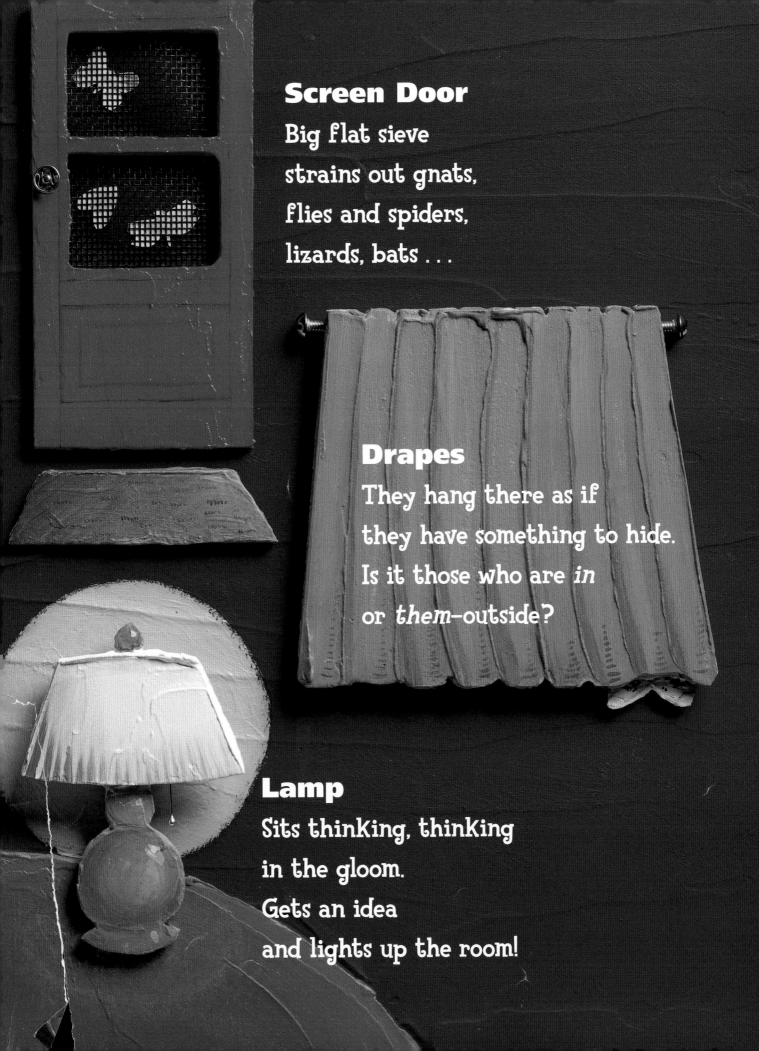

Screen Door

Big flat sieve
strains out gnats,
flies and spiders,
lizards, bats . . .

Drapes

They hang there as if
they have something to hide.
Is it those who are *in*
or *them*-outside?

Lamp

Sits thinking, thinking
in the gloom.
Gets an idea
and lights up the room!

Table

Nothing will put her
in such a good mood
as people around her
and plenty of food.

Houseplants

They creep around
as thick as thieves
whispering secrets
through vines and leaves.

Television

Full of surprises
costumes, disguises.
A magical box
that *hypnotizes*.

Clock

Changes at a steady pace
as time passes
across his face.

Couch

Friendly chap
with a big soft lap.

Tub

As a rule
she's hard and cool.
But warm and *splashy*
when she's full.

Bed

Wants to be hugged
every night.
Wants to snuggle
and hold someone *tight*.

Night-Light

Gladly glows
because he knows
he makes things safe
for eyes to close.

Good Night House

Happy in every
board and beam,
House dreams
her favorite
dream.

For Marielle
–D.L.

For Catherine
(sorry about the paint
on the dining room table)
and Grayson, with love
–D.C.

THIS IS A BORZOI BOOK PUBLISHED BY ALFRED A. KNOPF, INC.
Text copyright © 2000 by Dee Lillegard. Illustrations copyright © 2000 by Donald J. Carter.
All rights reserved under International and Pan-American Copyright Conventions.
Published in the United States of America by Alfred A. Knopf, Inc., New York,
and simultaneously in Canada by Random House of Canada Limited, Toronto.
Distributed by Random House, Inc., New York.

KNOPF, BORZOI BOOKS, and the colophon are registered trademarks of Random House, Inc.

Library of Congress Cataloging-in-Publication Data
Lillegard, Dee.
Wake up house! : rooms full of poems / by Dee Lillegard ; illustrated by Don Carter.
p.   cm.
Summary: Thirty-four poems which personify household objects from the bedroom window that
greets the sun's morning rays to the night-light that watches over sleeping dreamers.
1. Dwellings—Juvenile poetry. 2. House furnishings—Juvenile poetry. 3. Children's poetry, American.
[1. Dwellings—Poetry. 2. House furnishings—Poetry. 3. American poetry.]
I. Carter, Don, 1958– , ill. II. Title.
PS3562.I4557W3 2000
811' .54—dc21   99-33420

www.randomhouse.com/kids

ISBN 0-679-88351-7 (trade)
ISBN 0-679-98351-1 (lib. bdg.)

Printed in Hong Kong

March 2000
10 9 8 7 6 5 4 3 2 1